D0786251

＊ ＊ ＊

For Dillon and Sloane—may your lives be filled with hootenannies,
yippee ki-yays, and spurs a-jinglin'!
—M. S.

For Terry Copher—a true cowboy and friend.
—A. H.

＊ ＊ ＊

*The art for this book was created using watercolor paints
on Arches hot press watercolor paper, and finished in ink.*

Library of Congress Cataloging-in-Publication Data

Sadler, Marilyn.
Alice from Dallas / by Marilyn Sadler ; illustrated by Ard Hoyt.
pages cm
Summary: Two young cowgirls in Dallas, Pennsylvania, have a showdown on the school playground.
ISBN 978-1-4197-0790-2 (alk. paper)
[1. Cowgirls—Fiction. 2. Friendship—Fiction.] I. Hoyt, Ard, illustrator. II. Title.
PZ7.S1239Ah 2013
[E]—dc23
2012036740

Text copyright © 2014 Marilyn Sadler
Illustrations copyright © 2014 Ard Hoyt
Book design by Maria T. Middleton

Printed and bound in China
10 9 8 7 6 5 4 3 2 1

Abrams Books for Young Readers are available at special discounts when purchased in quantity for
premiums and promotions as well as fundraising or educational use. Special editions can also be
created to specification. For details, contact specialsales@abramsbooks.com or the address below.

ABRAMS
THE ART OF BOOKS SINCE 1949
115 West 18th Street
New York, NY 10011
www.abramsbooks.com

Marilyn **Sadler**

Illustrated by
Ard Hoyt

ALICE
FROM
★ DALLAS ★

ABRAMS BOOKS FOR YOUNG READERS ★ NEW YORK

lice was a spunky little cowgirl from Dallas. Every morning she put on her cowgirl hat, slipped into her cowgirl boots, and buckled on her cowgirl spurs. She was ready for a hoedown, a roundup, and a showdown.

Alice wanted to be a *real* cowgirl.
She sang cowgirl songs.
She practiced using her lasso.
She rode a wild pony.

She even said "Yippee ki-yay!" when she herded her dog, Bessie, around the backyard.

But Alice wasn't a real cowgirl. And she didn't live in
Texas, either. She was just an ordinary little girl from
Dallas, Pennsylvania.

Every day Alice rode her pony, Nellie, to school.
She moseyed on down the hall with her cowgirl spurs a-jinglin'.
"Howdy, partners," she said to her classmates.

Alice knew all about the Wild West. One day in class, she acted out a cattle roundup. When she was finished, everyone stood up and clapped.

"I reckon I'm the only cowgirl in all of Pennsylvania," said Alice.

Then one day a new girl moved to town. Her name was Lexis, and she was from Texas.

Alice could hear the new girl's spurs jingling all the way down the hall. And when she walked into the room, her hat barely cleared the door. Alice could even smell the leather from her fancy cowgirl boots.

Lexis from Texas was a *real* cowgirl. And Alice from Dallas was worried.

That afternoon at recess, Lexis let everyone take turns riding her pony around the playground.

"His name is Blaze, and he's a real Shetland pony!" Lexis told them.

Lexis knew cowgirl sayings that Alice had never
heard before.

She was great with her lasso.

And by the end of the day, all of her classmates were singing the new cowgirl song that Lexis had taught them.

The next morning, when Alice galloped up to school,
Lexis's pony was tied to *her* tree.

When she walked into the classroom, Lexis was acting out a stagecoach holdup. All of her classmates were cheering. And when Alice went to hang up her hat, Lexis's hat was hanging on *her* hook.

Alice took Lexis's cowgirl hat and dropped it on the floor. "It's time we had a showdown," Alice told Lexis. "On the playground at high noon."

When the bell rang for lunch, Alice put on her hat, buckled on her spurs, and hopped on her pony.

"Hi ho, Nellie!" she shouted as she galloped onto the playground.

Everyone was gathered in a circle, so Alice trotted into the center. She pranced sideways, backwards, and in tight little circles. Then she galloped at full speed across the playground and jumped over the teeter-totter.

"Top that!" said Alice, tipping her hat to Lexis as Nellie took a bow.

Lexis swung her lasso over her head and let it go. It glided through the air in slow motion, dropping over a monkey bar post. Then she yanked the rope tightly as it snapped and quivered.

"Tumbling tumbleweeds," muttered Alice under her breath.

Alice was no match for Lexis and her lasso.
So Alice started dancing.

"This is a little dance called the Texas Two-Step!" she shouted. "That's a step to the right, and a clappity-clap, and a hop to the back, and a slappity-slap. One shuffle and a twirl, and I'm a dancing cowgirl!"

When Alice finally stopped dancing, a small cloud of dust settled around her.

"Cowgirl up," she told Lexis. "It's your turn."

Lexis stepped into the circle and started dancing.

"Um," stuttered Lexis, "that was a—a step to the left . . . no, right! And a clappity-slap . . . I mean clap! And a hop and a slappity-slap. Then a shuffle and a twirl, and a—a . . . *uh* . . . *oh* . . ."

Lexis began twirling out of control . . .
spinning around and around . . . until she
hopped . . . then flopped . . . to the ground.

"Ouch!" she cried as she pulled off her fancy cowgirl boot.
Everyone watched as Lexis's foot got bigger and bigger.
"I reckon that's gonna hurt a little," said Alice.

That night, Alice could not sleep. She tossed and turned on her cowgirl bedroll. She was worried about Lexis's foot.

The next day, Lexis's pony was not tied to the tree. Her hat wasn't hanging on the hook, either. Alice listened for the sound of her spurs coming down the hall, but Lexis never appeared.

Alice wanted to see Lexis. She needed to know that she was all right. So she decided to go for a visit.

"Whoa, Nellie!" Alice shouted when they got to her house.

When Lexis opened the door, Alice was happy to see her. She looked as pretty as a wagon. And her foot was much better, too.

"I'm sorry," said Alice. "It was all my fault. I was such a show-off at the showdown."

"Horsefeathers," said Lexis. "You're a darn tootin' good dancer!"

Alice had to admit, she *was* a pretty good dancer. But she was not very good with a lasso.

"I will teach you how to lasso," said Lexis, "if you teach me how to dance. Deal?"

"Deal!" said Alice.

"But first, let's ride, cowgirl!"

Alice reckoned there was room for more than one
cowgirl in Pennsylvania. So she and Lexis hopped up
onto their ponies and trotted off down the trail.

Alice learned a lot about Lexis that afternoon. She learned that she liked campfires and hootenannies. She learned that she was afraid of rattlesnakes and tumbleweeds. She learned that her great-great-grandfather was an outlaw. She learned that she liked to sleep out under the stars.

But the biggest thing Alice learned about Lexis that afternoon was that Lexis wasn't a real cowgirl. In fact, she was just an ordinary little girl . . .

. . . from Texas, Indiana.